Anansi and the Talking Melon

retold by Eric A. Kimmel
illustrated by Janet Stevens

Holiday House / New York

To Thomas and Timothy
—E.A.K.
To my friend, Gail
—J.S.

This story first appeared in *Spider: The Magazine for Children*

Text copyright © 1994 by Eric A. Kimmel
Illustrations copyright © 1994 by Janet Stevens
All rights reserved
Printed in the United States of America
First Edition
Library of Congress Cataloging-in-Publication Data
Kimmel, Eric A.
Anansi and the talking melon / retold by Eric A. Kimmel ;
illustrated by Janet Stevens.—1st ed.
p. cm.
Summary: A clever spider tricks Elephant and some other animals
into thinking the melon in which he is hiding can talk.
ISBN 0-8234-1104-4
1. Anansi (Legendary character)—Legends. [1. Anansi (Legendary
character) 2. Folklore—Africa.] I. Stevens, Janet, ill.
II. Title.
PZ8.1.K567Ano 1994 93-4239 CIP AC
398.24′52544—dc20
[E]

One fine morning Anansi the Spider sat high up in a thorn tree looking down into Elephant's garden. Elephant was hoeing his melon patch. The ripe melons seemed to call out to Anansi, ''Look how juicy and sweet we are! Come eat us!''

Anansi loved to eat melons, but he was much too lazy to grow them himself. So he sat up in the thorn tree, watching and waiting, while the sun rose high in the sky and the day grew warm. By the time noon came, it was too hot to work. Elephant put down his hoe and went inside his house to take a nap.

Here was the moment Anansi had been waiting for. He broke off a thorn and dropped down into the melon patch. He used the thorn to bore a hole in the biggest, ripest melon.

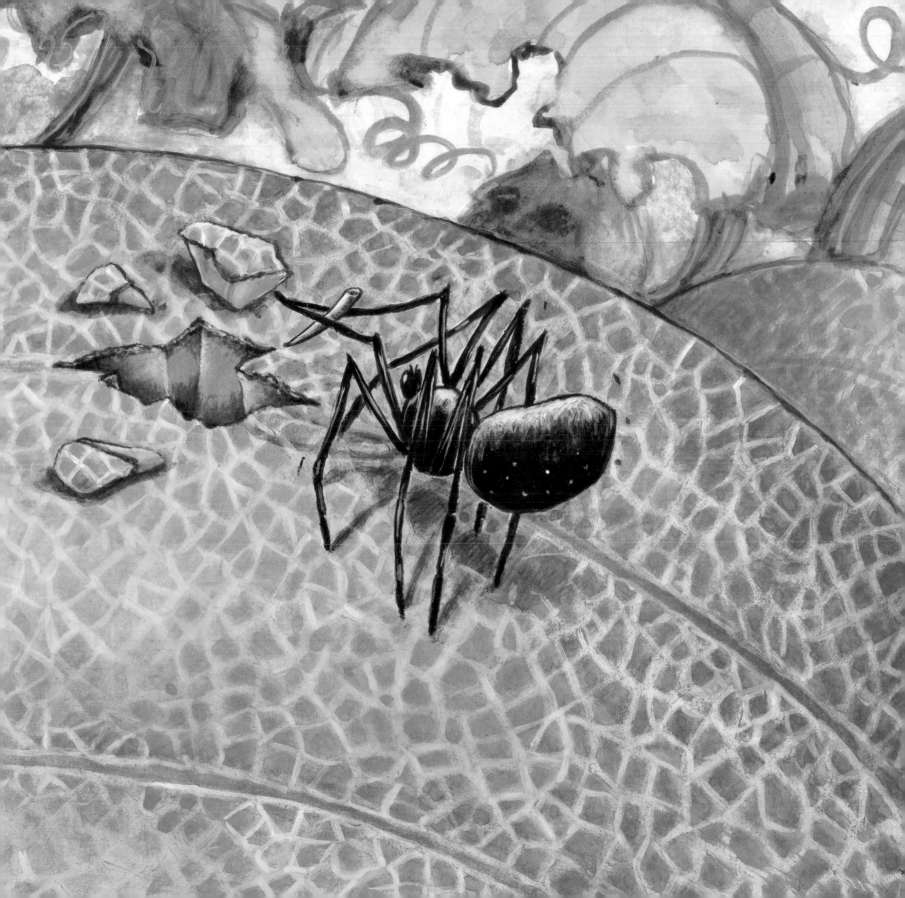

Anansi squeezed inside and started eating. He ate and ate until he was as round as a berry.

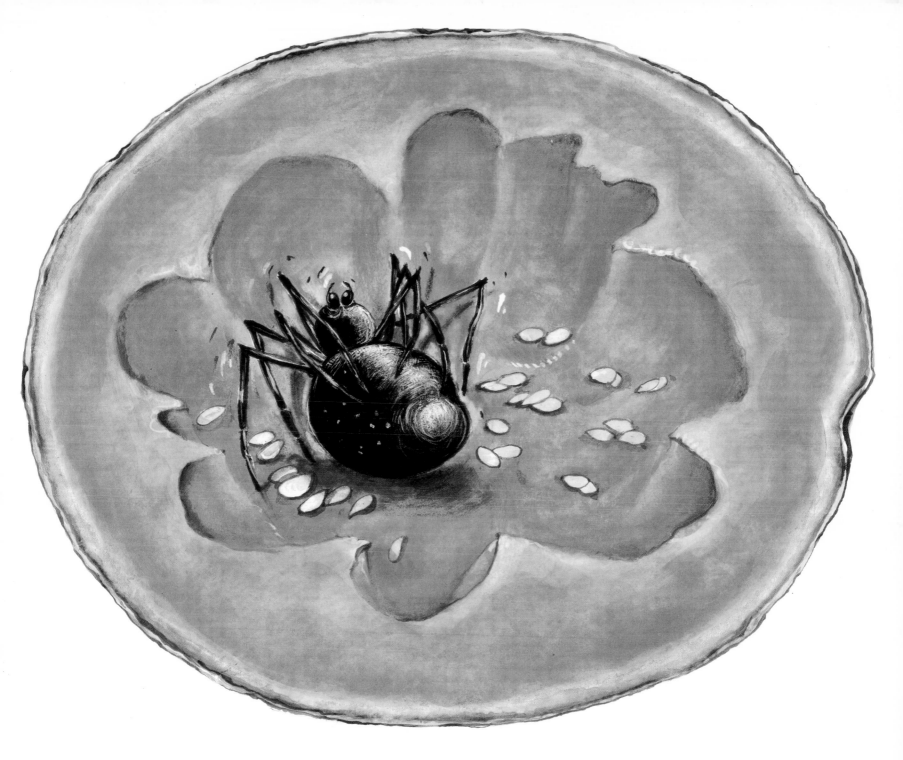

"I'm full," Anansi said at last. "Elephant will be coming back soon. It is time to go."

But when he tried to squeeze through the hole, Anansi had
a surprise. He didn't fit! The hole was big enough for a thin
spider, but much too small for a fat one.

"I'm stuck!" Anansi cried. "I can't get out. I will have to
wait until I am thin again."

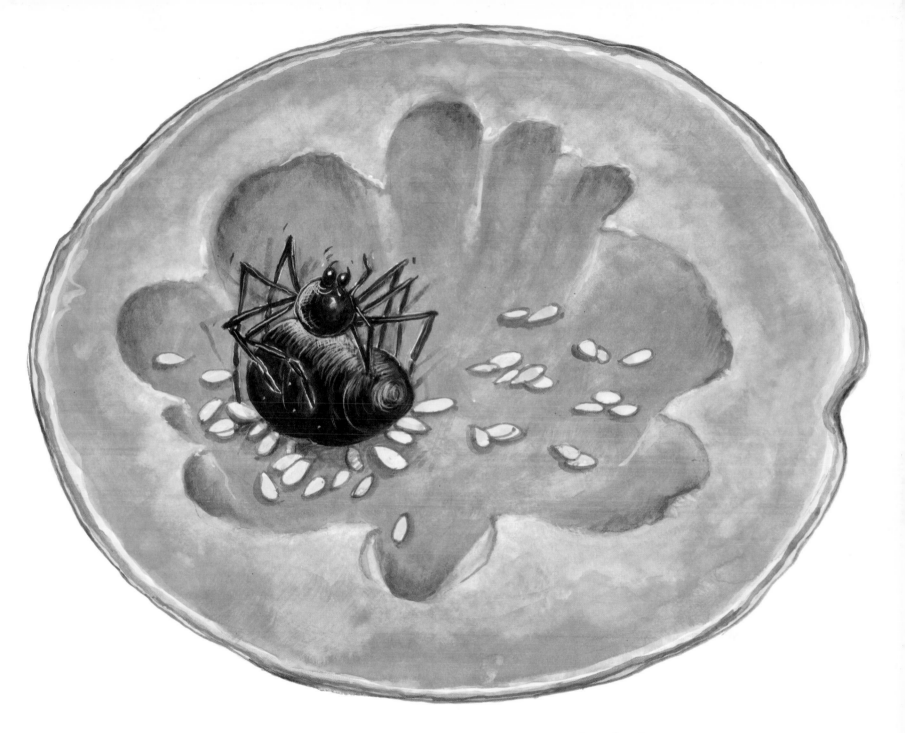

Anansi sat down on a pile of melon seeds and waited to get thin. Time passed slowly.

"I'm bored," Anansi said. "I wish I had something to do."

Just then he heard Elephant returning to the garden. Anansi had an idea. ''When Elephant gets closer, I will say something. Elephant will think the melon is talking. What fun!''

Elephant walked over to the melon patch. ''Look at this fine melon. How big and ripe it is!'' he said, picking it up.

"Ouch!" cried Anansi.
Elephant jumped. "Aah! Who said that?"

"I did. The melon," Anansi said.

"I didn't know melons could talk," said Elephant.

"Of course we do. We talk all the time. The trouble is, you never listen."

"I can't believe my ears!" Elephant exclaimed. "A talking melon! Who could believe it? I must show this to the king."

Elephant ran down the road, carrying the melon with An- ansi inside. Along the way, he ran into Hippo.

"Where are you going with that melon?" Hippo asked.

"I'm taking it to the king," Elephant told him.

"What for? The king has hundreds of melons."

"He doesn't have one like this," Elephant said. "This is a talking melon."

Hippo didn't believe Ele- phant. "A talking melon? What an idea! That's as ridic- ulous as . . ."

". . . a skinny hippo," the melon said.

Hippo got so angry his face turned red. "Who said that? Did you say that, Elephant?"

"It wasn't me. It was the melon," Elephant said. "I told you it talks. Do you believe me now?"

"I do!" Hippo exclaimed. "I want to go with you. I want to hear what the king says when you show him this talking melon."

"Come along, then," said Elephant. So Elephant and Hippo went down the road together, carrying the melon.

By and by, they ran into Warthog. "Where are you taking that melon?" Warthog asked them.

"We're taking it to the king," Elephant and Hippo told him.

"What for? The king has hundreds of melons," Warthog said.

"He doesn't have one like this," Hippo replied. "This melon talks. I heard it."

Warthog started to laugh. "A talking melon? Why, that's as ridiculous as . . ."

". . . a handsome warthog," said the melon.

Warthog got so angry he shook all over. "Who said that? Did you say that, Elephant? Did you say that, Hippo?"

"Of course not!" Hippo and Elephant told him. "The melon talks. Do you believe us now?"

"I do!" cried Warthog. "Let me go with you. I want to see what the king does when you show him this talking melon."

So Warthog, Elephant, and Hippo went down the road together, carrying the melon.

Along the way, they met Ostrich, Rhino, and Turtle. They didn't believe the melon could talk either until they heard it for themselves. Then they wanted to come along too.

The animals came before the king. Elephant bowed low as he placed the melon at the king's feet.

The king looked down. ''Why did you bring me a melon?'' he asked Elephant. ''I have hundreds of melons growing in my garden.''

''You don't have one like this,'' Elephant said. ''This melon talks.''

"A talking melon? I don't believe it. Say something, Melon." The king prodded the melon with his foot.

The melon said nothing.

"Melon," the king said in a slightly louder voice, "there
is no reason to be shy. Say whatever you like.
I only want to hear you talk."

The melon still said nothing. The king grew impatient.

"Melon, if you can talk, I want you to say something. I command you to speak."

The melon did not make a sound.

The king gave up. "Oh, this is a stupid melon!" he said.

Just then the melon spoke. "Stupid, am I? Why do you say that? I'm not the one who talks to melons!"

The animals had never seen the king so angry. "How dare this melon insult me!" he shouted. The king picked up the melon and hurled it as far as he could.

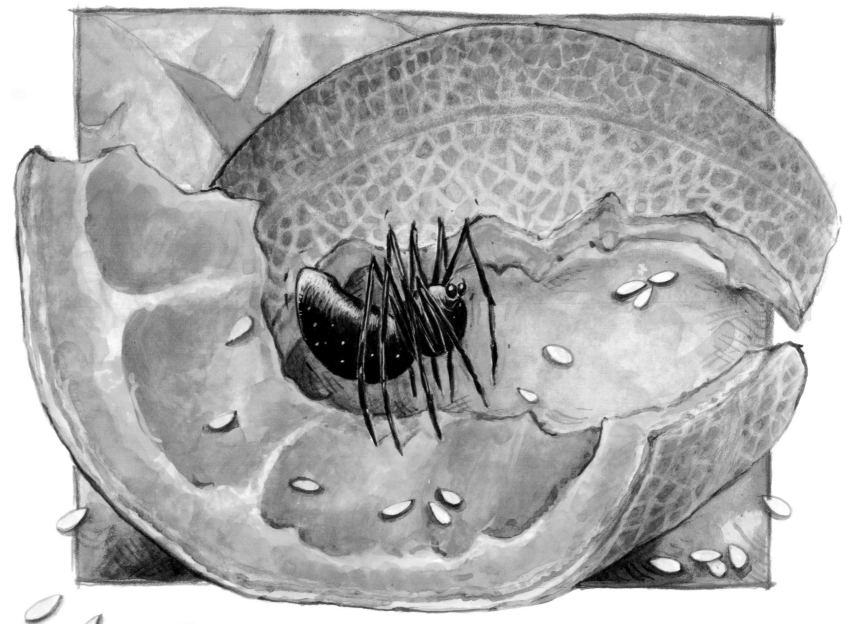

The melon bounced and rolled all the way to Elephant's house. KPOM! It smacked into the thorn tree and burst into pieces. Anansi picked himself up from among the bits of melon rind.

All the excitement had made him thin. And now that he was thin again, he was hungry. Anansi climbed the banana tree. He settled himself in the middle of a big bunch of bananas and started eating.

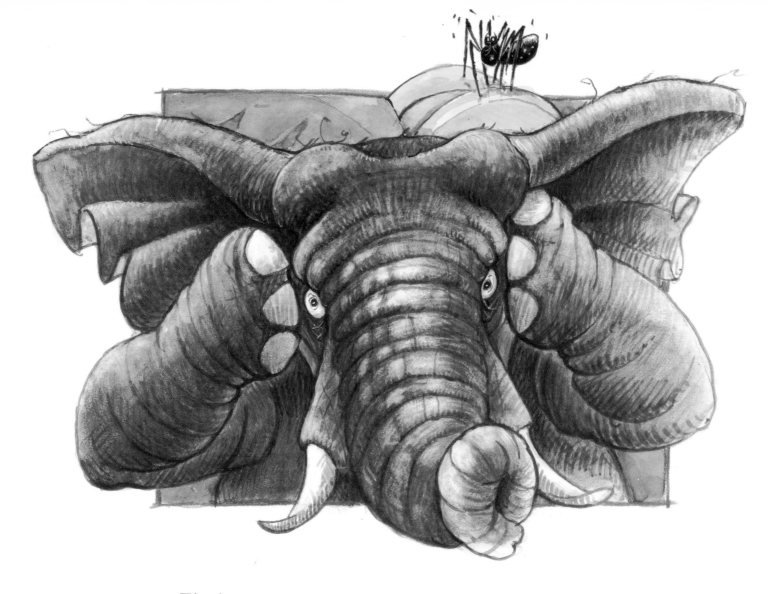

Elephant returned. He went straight to the melon patch.

"You melons got me in trouble with the king!" Elephant said. "From now on, you can talk all you like. I'm not going to listen to a word you say!"

"Good for you, Elephant!" Anansi called from the bananas. "We bananas should have warned you. Talking melons are nothing but trouble."